SILENCE

Silence

P.B. Lindberg

Contents

A Word from The Author

I wrote and published my first novel over five years ago. I was a young seventeen-year-old writer with ambitions of becoming a real author, to follow the calling I had received years prior. It took me five years of writing, inventing countless characters, writing thousands upon thousands of pages, and experimenting with numerous short stories to finally reach this point; to be able to present a worthy story to you, my dear reader.

There was a time when the younger P.B. Lindberg would have declared, "Woe is me, for I have not published a single work in five years." Yet, now I see the importance of those five years of dedicated practice. As a good friend of mine remarked, it was more than vital for me to be able to focus on sharpening my craft and writing, for it has finally brought forth good fruit.

This story is the product of rigorous thinking and contemplation. It not only required careful consideration for the language used, but it compelled me to gaze into the inner workings of the mind and see what darkness it can shelter and to observe what kind of tyranny it can lay upon the man who has yet to understand his own psyche. Thus, this story speaks to me profoundly, and I am certain we can all under-stand the struggle of Mr Soren. I hope this story shall speak to you in a meaningful way and reveal something new about yourself, and the world.

    - **P.B. Lindberg**

To my good friend, who aided me immensely in the editing of this work.

Silence, a restlessly held breath of nature, crept on the walls of a bleak house. It was harsh like black smoke, a suffocating cloud of mild poison, impossible to clear with a word of kindness. It was this silence that had conquered this humble apartment in London decades ago, and it had lived on the walls like moss on a rock, sprouting and strangling all around itself. If one were to harken his ears, he might have been able to hear a distant, distorted note of a piano, for its shadow still lingered in the corner, but it was merely a flicker of a voice long faded.

Yet, as unnatural and strange as it was, there was a soul in the room, neither fully faded into the grey tapestry, nor fully alive. He sat in a dusty armchair, gazing out the single tall window as pipe smoke hovered high onto the ceiling, where years of tobacco habit had created a sphere of tar and taint. A guest would have been forgiven were he to assume the man was indeed dead, for so little did he move or make any gesture asserting his hold to life. He was a statue of salt stone, a monument to callousness; every beating of his heart quivered before the quiet hissing of his pipe.

It was early in the morning and the sun was climbing high, painting the sky blooming yellow, crimson red, and royal blue. The light slowly descended into the room, illuminating the man's features, yet only slightly, for his bushy and time-beaten brows still held a veil of darkness over his face. His skin, parched and gnawed by frost, revealed him to be in his fifties. His head had strings of white hair still holding onto life and his wry face had a well-trimmed moustache as its single jewel, though it too tilted downwards, mournfully following the line of his lips. One could almost see the way his mouth moved ever so lightly, as if he was in a confessional, whispering hidden words from the depths of his spirit. Yet, it was clear by the shadow on his face that his heart was not truly speaking and whatever he might have whispered now, he had uttered a million times before.

There were certain oddities with the man, for he seemed as frigid as a bone, yet owned an aura of peculiarity, even frightfully so. He appeared unbreachable by the vulgar folk, unreachable by the normal world. His gestures, as few as there were of them, were done as if he were a cleric performing a ritual. The way he lightly tapped his pipe, the way he drew in the smoke, even the way his brows lifted slightly from time to time, allowing his glassy eyes to see the sun; all of this was performed with nearly unnatural formalness, a curious, yet terrifying strictness.

To whom was he performing these rites, these strange and ghastly gestures of life long faded? No one could tell and it was likely that even he shared the ignorance of the others. Yet so he remained an hour, perhaps two. The sun mounted the skies, the clock soon marched onwards to dampen the light, and the city of London was soon fully awakened, prepared to face its usual hurry and delightful chatter; chatter, which never breached the fort of his house.

His pipe died out, and he let out a final sigh. He drew three times and tasted the empty air with a cold aroma of tobacco. His brows lifted with trifle wonder, as if was surprised by this event every morning. He laid down his pipe and took three deep breaths, his eyes closing and hiding his troubled intellect behind his wrinkled eyelids. He then stood and marched to the kitchen, his steps precise, stern, and valiant in direction. One could nearly note the path that had formed on the carpet as if he never roamed off it.

The silence was disturbed as he prepared himself a cup of tea. He chose the same old mix of black teas he had consumed every morning. This variety of tea might not have surprised his tongue with new tastes or aromas, but it offered him another rite, another comfort of order. He stood by and stared at the teapot, counting time as his brows descended to further shadow his face. He waited, still like a mountain until it was done. He then poured himself a cup and added just the correct amount of milk. He stirred the concoction three times, tapped his spoon on the side, and took one sip, as always. He was prepared to enter his study.

The door was closed, as it always was, and a dim gloom hovered over it. He took a breath before entering and grimaced as if he was once again taken by surprise by the open shutters, through which the sun now beamed with unwelcome lustre. He considered rebuking himself for leaving the shutters open, yet he had done so for years, for his nocturnal pursuits had to be watched over by the belt of stars, and the crown jewel of heaven, the moon.

He had never had the mind to shut such a sight off, for so few were the glimmers of life in his own. Thus, after being reconciled with himself by his eternal error, he crossed the room, walking on a heavy carpet of washed brown tone. He laid his cup on the desk and fixed the knot of his tie before finally being seated. As he did, the silence returned and it crept into the home like a thief in the night. He lifted his eyes at the door as if to rebuke the silence which moved like a shadow. If silence could own a form, it would have trembled by his gaze, yet it continued on its quest, with silent steps.

The desk had towers of books on it, each tower constructed with similarly sized tomes. There were creme-coloured papers, some bare and sorrowful, some full of dark cursive, akin to the writings of the Middle Ages. There was a lamp the man turned on, but only after clearing space for his work.

The illumination allowed him to witness disappointment. His dim brown eyes read through the scribings, while his brows tightened in distaste. He rid himself of the sour writings by hiding the pages in a folder, bulky like an old Bible. He meticulously made sure the papers inside were sharply organised, strictly ordered before he stood and placed the folder on the vast bookshelf which stood by the longest wall, covering it in its entirety. It was then among many, amidst countless fellow folders without colour, covered by a blanket of dust and neglect. The shelf also housed countless books, most from the great writers the man had once eagerly read. Now the shelf was more akin to a morgue, for it rarely gained a new addition, if not counting the usual piece of rejected writings. The shelf had also taken upon itself features familiar to the man, for its appearance was also cast into shadow; the once rich texture of the wood had lost its beautiful shades and what remained was a giant of callous construction, a mere holster of long faded wonders and dreams.

The man studied the shelf for a time, as he always did. His lips remained as sharp as a sword, his posture straight as that of an officer, and his eyes gazed over the titles of the books, his mind muttering out their names from memory. He then returned to his desk and sat, dipped his pen in ink and wrote. He wrote testaments, reports of whatever he recalled sensing before. He wrote for an hour, then another, then another, until a few pages had been tainted by grim curves and sharp endings. It was then that he glanced at his pocket watch and realised it was reaching ten in the morning. His stomach let out a quiet notice of its compulsion and his mind answered with the thought of a familiar restaurant.

Thus, as he always did, he dimmed the light, returned his cup to the kitchen, and made his way to the narrow vestibule. He donned his grey overcoat, the very same he had used in his youth (the few dust-covered photos on the walls testified to this), buttoned it with care, and put on his grey hat before inspecting himself in the mirror. His aura was as grey as his garments, his face as joyful as harsh pavement. Yet his spirit was undisturbed and after the same fixes he repeated daily, he deemed himself fit to leave the comforting silence and enter the storm of chaos of the outside world.

II

The streets of London had already been afflicted by noise and the constant rustling of chatter. Commuters rushed to trams; children ran around attempting to flee the eventual beginning of school. The shops were open and over the city skyline shone the all-seeing sun, beaming down from its throne, casting out a cool wind upon the citizens.

Yet there came a dark cloud, conjured out of thin air. The root of it was an old man, gentleman in appearance, cynic by his features. He marched on the street with his hands firmly behind his back, his eyes studying the pavement, noting the new cracks and pieces of rubbish which made him shake his head and sigh with silent ire.

The children found the man curious, from afar that is, for when he approached, they fled with a playful scream. The man-made no gesture of note, instead, he marched onwards as if he was still partly asleep and was merely moving by the power of his memory. Yet he did make his usual observations about the people around him, about the city, most vitally about the new stains it had gotten and how ruination was slowly withering away the entire world.

In a manner most ritualistic, the man passed by a humble restaurant, one he had frequented for many years now. He inspected the menu of the day, grunted, and bid himself to return, as it was his tradition. He then continued on his way, until he arrived at a quiet park, with stout and lush sentinels standing guard, extending their arms over the gracefully attended fields of grass.

His boots gnarled against the gravel path, his eyes causing the earth to bow in reverence. He marched past the marble fountain, which still fulfilled its duty, tinkling sprays of water onto the pool below and onto some of the stones that housed tiny disks of moss on them. He journeyed through the park without lifting his eyes, and only after reaching the exit and entering a narrow pathway by the sea, did his eyes finally wake from their contemplated stupor.

A bay opened before him, the adventurous waves glistening in the golden sun, while ships came and went on their merry way. Crowds of workers, like ants from this distance, attended the ships and the cargo, no doubt bringing some strange goods from America, he thought.

The wind was cool, holding in itself the scent of salt and water. It was one of the few occasions when the overwhelming smell of dust, books, and tobacco was displaced, even for a moment that is, and indeed, the man stood long, watching the commotion with a familiar alienation. He saw a passenger vessel setting sail and felt his lips suddenly aching and there was a muffled pain in his chest.

He stood as if a portrait was being painted of him. His stoic face could have been misunderstood as a mere moment of a sudden gloom, yet it was indeed his natural state of being.

He squinted his eyes as the cold wind blew from the sea and he wondered where the ship was to sail to. Perhaps that America again? Maybe France? Perchance the vessel would soon meet the shores of Italy? He knew not, but the longer he allowed his mind to revel in the thought, the heavier his heart weighed within the chambers of his chest. Time seemingly ceased passing and for a moment he gazed over a sea of shadows, where no life could be seen, only the regretful waves that had now lost their golden sheen. He had to rescue his eyes from the sight and turned away, sighing.

The trees loomed over him, nearly bowing to him, taking part in his regular sorrow. The leaves rustled in the wind and a lonely seagull let out a desolate screech before fading under the splashing of the waves.

Thus, he set forth towards the restaurant. His watch alarmed him of the time, for it was approaching eleven, and his stomach quietly restated its appetite. He wasn't an idolatry man of cuisine, yet he often sought comfort in the episode of lunching, for it allowed him to step outside without having to face the insolent faces of the crowd.

He marched promptly to the restaurant and took his regular place on an elevated platform, just behind the corner where most customers wouldn't torment him with their eyes. He recalled hearing an old waiter, a man who once was of his age, greeting him whenever he used to enter, calling him by name.

He hadn't replied for a long time, but only after the man's constant infringement on silence had become a routine, did Mr Soren reply with a nod and a word muttered through a veil of thought. Then again, that was how it used to be, for now, there were no familiar unfamiliar faces and no sound.

He hung his coat in its usual place, fixed his collar, and took a seat, feeling the sun nibbling at his back through the dusty window. There were only a few crackles of sound in the air, yet no chatter, no overbearing speech over a meal. It was not unusual in this establishment, perhaps being the reason he favoured it over all others. A waitress soon came and took his order, his mind wandering in caverns far disconnected from the grey reality of the moment, and what came of his act of placing an order was simply an act of instinct.

He found himself staring at the same corner he had a habit of inspecting. A humble spider had grown its webbings to a large and intricate decal, and the tapestry, most familiar to the styles of Renaissance, seemed parched around the sharp corner. He had mapped the pattern through and through, yet his fresh joy, or the least regretful task, was watching the spider work on its craft. It added to the pattern of the wall while adding a layer of irregularity to it all. It made Mr Soren's lips nearly lift in a sense of irony and he only took his eyes off the spider after receiving his meal.

He ate without much thought, hearing bursts of noise here and there, often lifting his brow and casting a slight look of indignation around him. Usually, there had been an unfortunate customer who had received the spear of his eyes, but not today. It was nearly as quiet as in his house. It burned his gut with a flame of uneasy and anxious anticipation for something that was not there.

III

After the deed of lunching was completed in at least a satisfactory manner, Mr Soren returned home, his senses lulled into a brief moment of peace by the power of coffee and the soothing sun that graced his face. Yet it didn't take long for his thoughts to start marching again, and he soon fell into deep contemplation about matters he had resolved countless times. Such was the tradition of the court of his mind, and today's session had begun.

The quiet whistling of the wind, the chatter of the folk, the heart-aching singing of a lonely bird, all of the sounds were shut away as he closed the gate of his house and descended into the silence. For a brief time, he could hear his heart beating with anxious anticipation, but as he tilted his mind towards it, his heart cowered away and returned to its place.

He removed his coat in a manner most elegant, following the thread of instinct that led him towards his study. The odour of dusted tomes felt, as always, like burning coals in his nostrils, now that the wind had given him a point of comparison. But as he fell into his work, holding onto his pen like a sword glimmering with flame, his senses succumbed to his surroundings. Thus, the lights, the sounds, and the scents of the outside world were all forgotten, as if he had simply woken from a restless sleep. He scribed with a diligent effort of stoic perfection. No matter what he wrote, his face remained unwavering, stern, and coldly stable, as if he was merely a distant spectator, looking down upon the creative act like a judging father.

Yet in the back of his mind, far from the court of judges that now followed his work, lived a foreign thought, an exiled piece of his memory, a mere flicker of a reflection he had once witnessed in the mirror. It was a thought reminding him of a time he had written with a passion stronger than any love between folk, with a diligent discipline greater than any hero of the myths, with emotions that flowed through him like a weeping river, only to be channelled through the ink and onto that harsh creme-coloured paper. The thought was an evil affliction, the court reminded him, like an old wound that resisted any attempt of mending. Whenever he allowed the thought to enter the stage of his conscience, he simply scoffed at it and rebuked it with wrath and disappointment, like a mentor scolding his pupil. Yet no matter his harsh words, no matter the beatings he served at the thought, it held onto its position of narrow existence, never letting him fully rest in peace.

He wrote for three hours without speaking, without standing, without lifting his eyes off the paper. Precisely after the time had come, he glanced at his watch and allowed the thought of tea to break his concentration. He then ventured to the kitchen and supplied his intellect with a warm cup before returning to his work. He wrote for another three hours, after which he held in his hand a piece of paper, fit enough to survive through the flames of his judgement and the judgement of the court. It was this moment that came dangerously close to making him smile, even barely, yet he murdered the urge and cast it out like a wretched heretic. He then proceeded to study his work with utmost criticism, nodding before hiding it in a slightly less worn folder. It was time for his daily pilgrimage, his march of duty, his never-ending journey to nowhere and nothingness.

Time had flown and twilight was over the land. Witnessing the darkness entering his study was a comfort to him, akin to an old friend. Darkness, as he thought, cleansed the world of ugliness and he wore it like a cloak, to keep up the peace, the silence, and the order.

He fixed his attire, brushed his remaining hair and moustache, put on his coat, and left once again, abandoning his home to the will of silence. His footsteps echoed in the hallway until he finally reached the exit and saw the dark blue sky beckoning to him.

The air was cool like the fresh bite of winter, unwavering like a drawn string, and breathless with anticipation. The darkness rushed to him like a servant, bowed to him, and walked with him without a word. His steps felt like the distant knocks, echoing into the streets and alleyways. His eyes smote no people, for most had either wandered back home or entered the restaurants and pubs in search of vain comfort among their peers. As he passed the houses of the crowds, he could feel a quiet urge, like a ghost limb, urging him to gaze inside and fill his heart with poison, yet he paid no heed to the thought and hadn't done so in years.

He felt a sudden shiver, realising himself getting older by the second before falling into thought. The piece he held in his hand had become an abomination in the dark recesses of his intellect, for the court had reevaluated his work and come to find it less than satisfactory. Yet he knew he could not turn away now, for the giver of his livelihood demanded his scribings, no matter what he wrote. It was a simple and worthless act of transaction, which he had once excitedly waited for, yet now came to find as meaningless as the smiles around him.

He soon faced a tall building, grey and beaten by the elements. One would have been forgiven were he to assume the building had long been abandoned, but in fact, it still sheltered a collection of *intellectuals,* or naive self-idolatries, as he had titled them. Yet it was here where he left his piece, feeling as if he had once again given a piece of himself and abandoned it into the night, where wolves and other beasts waited, their eyes bleeding red with blood. Yet, after further thought, he struggled to recall whether the piece he now left was true of himself, or perhaps it was of some other man, one he had not known before. He stood a while, staring at the wooden door, waiting for an unknown force to open it and smite him with light. The trees close by hummed to him and a twirl of leaves brushed against his ankles. He turned and watched the leaves rush forth, nearly walking as a man would towards the park. Ah, yes, it was the last rite of the day, the one that should offer him the least discomfort.

He could see the lights of the peaceful bay through the tree line, and as he hearkened his ears, the sombre bubbling of the waters reached his senses in a solemn tone. The waters spoke to him words he had heard before.

He prepared the tobacco, lit it, and drew, watching the cloud of smoke fade into the dark sky. He closed his eyes for a brief moment, feeling the wind nibbling at his ears and the ground pushing up against his feet. He faded into the scenery, for a moment that is, free from the battle of thought that raged within him as often as his heart beat. Though the event was a humble one, one most people would never even consider an event, to him it offered one last bastion of solace, and he lifted his serious face to the sky and allowed his sight to fade into the dark around him. Tomorrow will be a new day. Tomorrow will repeat yesterday. Yet, at least he was now, for a moment, neither repeating nor anticipating a thing. He was free in silence, and as the darkness clothed him with its desolate power, he returned to his seat and fell into timelessness.

IV

Through the veil of darkness, the sea of silence, the gentle whisper of the wind, ascended a sound most foreign to him. At this hour, amidst the abyss, came quiet clicks of footsteps most light. They echoed some distance away, approaching him with an elegant rhythm and a strange sense of life. The steps entered the park, his sanctuary until they suddenly faded as if they never existed. Silence retook its throne and he was left to wonder, lifting his brow as he resisted the urge to open his eyes. Yet, he could not combat the sensation that was slowly burning his chest. The silence had gained a new form, an anxious nature that held its breath, waiting for it to be shattered. He opened his eyes and felt his face tense with pique.

At first, his vision remained blurred, dominated by the shadows that hung from the trees, but he soon realised there was a figure sitting just opposite to him. It was a woman, dressed in an embroidered white blouse and a creme-coloured dress. She appeared to illuminate with light, as if the fabric of her clothes were kin to the shining jewels of the sky.

A coolness most intoxicating washed over him and he

gave the woman an intrigued gander, yet couldn't see the woman's face, for the dark shielded her like a cavalier. As to calm his mind and keep the court from assembling, he lit another cigarette and drew in the smoke, his senses retreating to ponder the taste of tobacco and the touch of the smoke.

Her slender figure, glimmering like an angel fallen from a realm free of dark and the bite of frost. He noted her familiar gestures, her way of watching the world around her. She appeared as comfortable in the park as he did and whenever the wind ceased breathing, he could nearly hear her melancholic, yet vibrant sighs. Nonetheless, he awaited her to depart and lift her eyes off himself.

Yet, as the time threatened to reveal the falsity of his confidence, he began to ponder why a woman or her kind, or anyone for that matter, would wander out in a weather such as this, at a time like this. He felt a certain animosity within himself, as if the site most holy to him had been defiled and disturbed. The darkness he had trusted to shield him from the sight of the crowds had now failed him, and now, at the hour most quiet, he was disturbed by the constant scorching of another's eyes on him.

He held onto his intellect, his resolve not to give way to such thoughts that were obviously contrary to his better knowledge, yet as solemnly as he promised himself not to, he still glanced at the woman from time to time. It was a peculiar feeling, a spell that contrived the reality itself, and he felt his heart beating with an uncomforting vigour, conjured by a flame he had snuffed out decades ago.

Whenever he gazed upon the woman, hoping to cast a rebuke with his eyes, he instead found a spell being cast on himself. The woman gazed in turn upon him through the veil of darkness that still, to some effect, shielded his face. As the darkness gave way, he observed her drawing something in her notebook, her hand moving with the humble elegance of an artist. She would sit still, only allowing her hand to work before taking a glance at him from time to time. He could feel two glistening jewels inspecting him before suddenly vanishing again. This strange cycle repeated itself for a time that was not bound by the mortal understanding of it. The park had seemingly entered another plane, where the night would only end after one soul decided to stand.

It was at his third cigarette that she lifted her notebook and gazed upon it as if it were her newborn child. He could not but raise his brow and, to cut his suddenly rising smile, scoff, though a hidden voice spoke out a word deep from within his spiteful soul.

Why does this woman torment me so? Is all peace vanquished on this earth? Have I nowhere to go to be at peace?

As much as he hesitated to admit it, he was perhaps more intrigued than annoyed by her. Suddenly, he fell into a dark cavern of thought as his recollection of the entire day enforced a sense of oddity about the day. Had he woken on the wrong foot? Had he broken a sacred routine or insulted his traditions? As far as he could recall, he had done no such thing, yet why then was he being afflicted with an oddity such as this?

The woman tilted her head as she looked at him, for a time before her face lifted to view the dark sky. He lifted his cigarette and drew, his fingers trembling and his heart burning with a suffocating flame. The cigarette was soon snuffed out and he crunched it under his foot. The silence was still present, as was the darkness, but its nature had been defiled. It no longer remained blissfully around him, shielding him from the sights and pollution of the world. Instead, it now lingered like a wounded wolf, waiting for the inevitable, which was something his spirit could never accept.

He thus stood and resisted the urge to look upon her again. He managed to remain fast in his resolve until he reached the gate that led to the shore. He, or the young voice inside him, cast a spell on him which forced his head to glance at her. He saw her eyes again. They were deep like a clear ocean, glimmering like silvery diamonds, and on the other side, he saw something most beautiful, yet most terrifying. He could not name it, yet the mere event made his legs tremble and his heart forgot to uphold its eternal duty.

Suddenly, his body was struck with age, and he stumbled forward, grasping the railing and grunting. He felt sprinkles of water on his face and stared into the black depths, seeing his dark reflection floating on the waters.

Sorcery, a torment cast upon him by God, no doubt about it.

Disoriented, he lit another cigarette, though the quest took multiple matches to succeed due to his pale fingers. As soon as the tobacco was set alight, he drew in the smoke as if it were the source of all life. He drew, blew out the smoke, and watched it fade away without a shape or purpose. He drew, blew out the smoke, and witnessed it hovering towards a glimmering star that had risen brighter than its brethren.

He drew, blew out the smoke, and as the cloud disbanded, footsteps echoed from behind him.

His heart pulsed in his throat and on his lips hovered a venomous curse.

Leave me be, must all the wraiths of the world torment me, even in this crib of blissful darkness?

Yet the moon soon revealed its majestic beauty and the world was cast into a silvery sheen. A cascade of silvery light reached over the waters until they found refuge in her figure. She stood not far from him, gazing at the sea.

The wind stirred her long brown hair, and the lights of heaven illuminated her face. Now that he had the chance to gaze upon her in light, there came a realisation of her being something close to kin to himself. The aura which surrounded her was familiar to him in all its forms of coldness and isolation, yet the way her eyes glimmered instilled in him a doubt, a fear, a sensation more foreign to him than anything.

Nonetheless, a young voice in his mind, the one he had cast aside for what felt like an eternity, stepped forth, as if to present himself before a court of vengeful judges. His words were a pain to his mind, which instantly rejected them, but more so was it a red coal in his spirit.

His grip on the cool railing tightened and his jaw bit as if there was a stone between his teeth. There was a hastily battle in his mind and the young voice let out a gasp, but he soon crushed the revolt and order was established in the court. Whatever strange oddities, and emotions, he had experienced, he was quick to exile to their usual place. Yet he could not rein in his heart, which still tilted in an unusual direction and beat with irregularity that threatened to turn him mad.

Then, a voice through the veil, a word of curious apology. It was quiet enough to be nearly swallowed by the waves, yet powerful enough to break the walls of quiet in his mind. He couldn't but turn to her, realising she was now merely a few feet from him.

Her face, aged, soft, and painted with timeless memories of sorrow, was bright and covered with a flame that seemingly had its source within her. It was a fantastical sight, yet as harshly as he tried, he could not silence his heart's verdict of her being beautiful.

She gave a word of anxious apology for disturbing him. Though her hands made a shiver as she fixed her white cotton gloves, her face slowly radiated with a warmer smile. She inquired for his permission to draw him, giving a flustered laugh, noting the beautiful scenery all around them.

His spirit was, for a moment, cast out from the clutches of his physical form. In its stead, confusion, quiet and disturbed, revealed its presence in his face. He remained stern, yet his slightest of gestures showed his bewilderment.

He mustered the strength to speak, alerting his intellect to judge his voice so as not to sound unnecessarily callous or too eager, for in truth, he did not know where he stood in the matter. He gave her permission and began anxiously waiting if her pen would steal his soul on paper.

She smiled with relief, her face washed with the light of the moon. She took a step back, sought support from the railing, and began sketching. He resumed his original posture and sought to clear his mind by staring at the bay, yet as usual as the sight was for him, it was now cast into imbalance by the constant beating of another heart; his own was, as much as possible, quiet like a disciplined child, yet in every thud there was an eagerness to join her rhythm.

She soon ceased her work and gazed upon her creation with apparent gladness. She thanked him with a slight courtesy and asked for his name.

Silence conquered the air around them and even the waters halted their eternal dance. He frowned and looked at her with hidden turmoil, as if he didn't speak her language. His eyes were burning like dry timber, but as he watched her ever-smiling face, he realised his error with a shock of embarrassment.

Mr Soren.

He granted a slight nod and faced the sea, as if attempting to flee from her.

She quietly voiced her surprise and asked whether or not he was one of the writers in the local paper. Her words had a form of eagerness most unfamiliar to him, and though his lips had nearly melded shut, he soon replied that he indeed held such a position.

Her lips lifted, as did her entire figure, as if her spirit had been reinvigorated, and she revealed that she had come across some of his writings and had fancied many of them, especially the ones he had written earlier in his time. She spoke with the sweetness of honey and the warmth of a familiar fireplace in winter. There was no hint of pride, of the common sounds of ingenuine utterings. He found it increasingly difficult to remain reserved and true to his nature, all the while the young voice reemerged despite his earlier efforts.

After mustering up the will, he thanked her for her kind words, nodding. They remained silent for a moment before he, forced by the young voice in his mind, asked for her name in turn, for courtesy's sake.

Ms Phoebe.

Their eyes avoided one another for a time until the silence grew too terrible and they gazed into one another's souls. Her face had turned beautifully red, like leaves during fall, and in those eyes, he saw as if another sea twinkled, crowned with a belt of stars. He felt himself fading from reality, losing his grasp on his very nature. He felt as if he was about to fall into a pit of unknown fires and was powerless to avoid the fall.

He glanced at his watch and remarked about the time. After a brief interaction, they both realised living around the same part of the city and, once again urged by the ever-strengthening young voice, he asked for the privilege of walking the lady home. One of his pretences was to see what she had drawn. She claimed the need to work on the piece but would be willing to present it to him at a later date, if he was interested.

Thus, they walked by the sea, until the path forced them to enter the dead-silent street. There were no words between them, only a few glances that sought for something unknowable and unreachable. His heart weighed heavily, cast into a fire he had dreaded all his life, yet he found himself surrendered to it and he could witness himself walking with her, as if his *true* self had been cast out, left to stare at the scene like a raven in the sky.

At her door, they made quiet remarks about their unusual meeting. She inquired if he wanted to meet her at the local cafe in a few days, for it would be then when she could share her drawings with him. He agreed, though in his mind he heard the court roaring in terror, demanding him to stop. Yet so it was that they departed, her face blushing and his face red, with cold sweat running down his temples. His features, cold and stoic, trembled under the weight of this newfound unfamiliarity, this fresh oddity, a factor of intrusive randomness. Yet the young voice, speaking from his heart, gave a word in her defence and urged him to cast out the thought already conjured in his mind; the thought of not meeting her a second time.

He walked home in the dark, feeling himself as hidden as a city on a hill. His mind felt foreign to him as if the train of his thought had been conquered by strangers, leaving him with little to do in protest. Yet his heart beat with a quiet warmth, and thus he returned home, neither with a word nor with total silence.

V

The night was restless with a constant whispering of the void and the mumblings of a mind. Voices, vastly different in character, yet sharing a host, came forth to announce their judgement, their carefully crafted pieces of wrath. He laid in bed, his eyes wide open, yet overshadowed by exhaustion. The ceiling appeared to flee from him as his mind was slowly falling into its own strife. It soon began and the court recalled the foul occurrence that had taken place just some hours ago, their analytics leaving nothing to mystery, nothing to be left in the dark, yet first came the more than familiar rebukes directed at him.

Why did you break your silence? Why did you share your words with a woman of her kind? Are you mad? Do you wish to make yourself a complete and utter fool?

Such was the discourse of his mind and for the time being there was no sign of the young voice who had so led him to take this foolish action. But, contrary to all normality, the court came to a sudden halt as he fell into a troubled sleep. Yet at the final moments of his conscience, he knew the trouble would most certainly continue and he accepted it without a grievance entering his mind. This, after all, was simply how he functioned.

When he woke up, he felt a hollow cavity in his chest, as if his spirit had still remained asleep. Over him loomed a dizziness and an alarm, as if the dark surrounding him had suddenly turned against him. He glanced around himself, his back against the wall, his face full of stale suspicion. He remained braced, prepared for a quick attack, an ambush to come from the depths and devour him, yet nothing happened and as the air around him turned brighter, he could only hear his uneasy breaths and the distant ticking of a clock.

He clothed himself and sat in his armchair, preparing his pipe and setting the tobacco aflame. Usually, his mind would obey his desire for silence and keep the chaos of thought still for the duration of his smoke. Yet today was afflicted with strangeness most uncanny, for the storm of his mind, the chaotic court of his intellect, resumed their tiring duty with haste. His mind was entrenched in a furious argument, and no odour, no taste of tobacco, no thought of worldly joys, could soothe him.

Nonetheless, he followed his routine to the letter, smoking, thinking, and simply observing his mind babbling as the world outside slowly awakened from its rest and burst into exasperating life. He felt himself more silent than usual, while indeed it was his mind that raged with a storm of voices. He stood as if on thin ice, his feet nearly breaking the thin foundation of his life. It was as if an evil deity, a god, a demon, was observing him, listening to the court fall into despair. He gazed into the sky and wondered whether or not he had merely dreamed the events of last night, for it had always been a challenge to differentiate the days from another.

By the end of his smoke, his intellect had come to a nearly unanimous verdict. Indeed he, Mr Soren, had spoken to a strangely curious woman and thus had made himself a visible fool. The judges reminded him of the disorder, the deadly poison of people, yet amongst their voices stood one the court dreaded the most. It was the one who spoke to him yesterday, a young man with a voice he knew better than the one he used to utter his few words. The voice congratulated him for his courage, yet his words were like whispers, spoken under the watchful eye of the court. As he laid down his pipe, it was this voice who managed to remind him to meet the woman today before noon, as arranged yesterday.

This enraged the court and as he prepared himself a cup of tea, his mind had indeed fallen into a flaming debate, drowning any sense of clarity or purpose. He sighed with years of grievances shaking his voice, bringing the cup to his lips, and allowing the warmth to wash through him. He would return to the thought later, but there was work to be done.

Yet as he sat in his study, inspecting papers with a pen in hand, he couldn't but feel his heart beating distressingly, nagging him about the passage of time. His hand trembled, aching to scribe a word onto the page, yet his mind refused to grant the order. Instead, he found himself considering the words he would have to utter when he inevitably met her again, and indeed, he soon found himself staring blankly at the wall, his mind conjuring scenarios of the upcoming trial.

Why did you give your word so foolishly?

At times, he felt the most unnatural urge to strike his fist against the desk and shout out a curse, yet his brows only knitted themselves together and he sealed his lips as if to snuff out the flame that was about to engulf him with rage. Nonetheless, his rite was defiled by the restless tapping of his finger, following the rhythm of his heart.

The time he would have spent working was instead spent on recalling yesterday, thinking about her. The court reminded him of the evils of people, painting her as another of the many, a detester of silence, a broker of peace, a jester of smiles. Yet the young voice countered and told him of the stars that shone in her eyes; such was the power of this thought that it shut out the court, at least for a brief moment in time.

He found himself sitting before legions of the public, his calm office, his peaceful sanctuary, now disturbed, threatened, made unstable. He found himself thinking thoughts that were not his own, hearing voices that he had either never met before, or thought to have died a lifetime ago. Yet, as the young voice asserted, perhaps it was all to be viewed as a good matter, instead of a terrible affliction.

But how could it be? Why would you find goodness from the crowd of licentious knaves?

Such was the thought that left him staring at his bookshelf, his eyes scanning the shadows that rested on the dusted tomes, the containers of worlds, of mere thoughts, flickers of reality past and future.

The time ultimately came when his work had to be set aside. She would be waiting and, on the count of his honour and dignity as a man, he had to fulfil what he, perhaps in his foolishness, promised. He entrusted himself to meet her, focus on the coffee and attempt to remain silent, then eat his lunch and return to work. This insurrection of stability would be a short-lived matter and his nature would be stabilised by the end of the day. Thus, despite the objections of the court, his mind was evened and the storm ceased, for now.

He fixed his tie, brushed his suit, and put on his coat. Perchance he fixed his tie one additional time, maybe he combed his moustache more carefully than before. Yet he rejected any notion of doing so, ignoring the court's suspicions.

I would never do such a thing, he proclaimed to the court.

The streets of London were unusually bright. The sun had, almost instantaneously, leapt to beam upon the land like a divinely appointed orb of flame, casting out shadows and sending out the wind to stir the air. He passed the places he always did, yet this time his mind was absent of the normal observations. His eyes didn't rise to smite the folk around him, to glance in annoyance at the laughing children, to look into the shops with a dark frown on his face. No, for now, his heart began beating with a resolve most unfounded in his life. He felt himself split, unable to grasp the true essence of his being, but what he could sense was his growing dread of the upcoming meeting. The closer he came to the realisation of the event, the louder the court protested, still demanding him to turn back.

He thought about the act of conversation and felt a sharp pain rolling in his chest. It would require speech, speech might lead him astray and make him give further promises, or worse, lay open the gates of his being. He swore not to let such a terrific event occur, but as he approached the cafe, he felt his old legs trembling, his gut burning, sweat welling from his temples. Before he entered, he wiped his face and studied himself in the reflection of the window, assuring himself one final time of his outward condition.

Yet, as he was fixing his appearance, silently berating himself regarding all possible matters, his eyes phased inward into the cafe and he saw Ms Phoebe. She appeared slightly timid as she studied her surroundings, yet she sat with utmost elegance, sipping her coffee with an aura of royalty. It wasn't long before their eyes met and, after her face gained a red hue, she beamed at him, granting a slight gesture of greeting. Her eyes were like spears in his spirit and, for a moment, he was stunned. He dwelled inward, forgetting his painfully lively surroundings as the grey world of his mind enveloped him. It was only the bell hanging on the door that woke him from his trance and he realised he was bound to enter; retreating was no longer possible.

He placed his usual order and marched to her. So swift, yet controlled were his actions that the court couldn't but sit idly and witness him doing the unthinkable. As she extended her hand, he took it gently and kissed it as a greeting. Before he could even sit down, the court had once again judged him for his foolishness, yet their voices were now like the distant buzzing of insects in the night.

She did bid him a blessed morning, joyfully remarking that she was beginning to consider the possibility of her arriving too early.

Her smile threatened the balance of his lips and as she partly hid herself behind her coffee cup, he felt a twitch on his face. His lips lifted into a short-lived smile and he remarked that the timing was more than satisfactory. The smile faded as his eyes fled from hers and, for a time, he studied the cafe around him with feigned interest.

The voices around the cafe then took the president and they sat there, avoiding one another's eyes, sipping their coffee in a predictable rhythm. She was red, her brown hair resting over her slender and lifted shoulders. He was pale, his lightly wrinkled face stringing from time to time as if it struggled to keep up its form. It was then that the young voice spoke in his mind and suggested he inquire about her art.

She blushed at his request and stammered her words before drawing out a notebook from her handbag. Through her slightly embarrassed demeanour, there was a clear sign of excitement, which she promptly hid underneath a required sense of charity. Her eyes were bright, peeking at him from time to time as she flipped through the pages, her fingers shivering as if a cold wind had bit them. She soon came across the correct page and she slid the notebook to him.

Something clicked in his heart, in his very spirit, for the art he now viewed stole his breath. His tensed figure felt a certain relief as he studied the marvellously drawn pieces. She had sketched him into the scenery in a beautiful manner and he noted how strangely difficult it was for him to recognise himself. Indeed, it was nearly impossible, for the way she had depicted him included a flame that had not burned within him in a lifetime. She complimented her art with an unusual genuineness and found her gazing away, twirling her hair. She, like any truly talented artist, explained that the piece was simply a first draft, but that she wished to paint it into a fully realised piece, if he would grant her the honour.

He gave her the right, resisting the urge to allow a new feeling to spread from the depths of his heart.

She was evermore radiant and thanked him with her eyes anxious to look at him. Everything else around the world appeared to fade, while the sun entered the cafe and lifted her figure, illuminating her with a halo of dusted gold.

Though it took them a while, they began discussing art in more detail. She explained her inspiration and her process of work before inquiring about his writing. Such was their conversation before they ventured from subject to subject, circling inwards and towards the depths of their spirits. At all times, the court willed to reject the matter, yet the young voice was now at the helm of his intellect and it urged him onward.

The two of them thus came to realise they had a lot in common, for they enjoyed similar books, music, and art. She also remarked that she frequented the same cafes, restaurants, and parks as he, which caused him to wonder how he had not seen her before. It was a most curious, yet disturbing thought that lingered in his mind for some time.

In an act that shocked him, he offered her lunch, if only she had the time. At first, she was slightly taken aback by the offer, but as her clear blue eyes studied his own, she accepted with delight most pure. They thus went and ate in the palace most usual to him, continuing their discussion about all manner of things, carefully and reservedly granting each other pieces of their true lives.

The longer they conveyed, the more he came to realise she

was akin to himself, and while his heart was beating with a longing, a desire newly found, his intellect was still troubled, casting a dark spell of soreness on his senses.

After their surprisingly joyful lunch, they took a short walk through the park they had met in. She expressed her glee in their newfound friendship, the mention of which stirred his very being with a nameless sensation, both foul and terrifyingly pleasant. They departed henceforth, both having to resume their work, but as he bid her farewell, holding her hand for a moment more, he felt as if he could be stunned right there and then, being cast into a void where he owned no form. The sight of her smile, her soft features radiating in the light of nature, burned his eyes, yet, contrary to all things he knew to be right, he did not look away.

It was only after he returned home that the court awakened from its silent stupor and recommenced the discussion. Time had flown, he had missed his routine and would thus remain unstable until the end of the day.

The court pondered the reasons for her sudden appearance, though they couldn't reach a verdict, not yet, for so strongly did his heart beat and still so firmly the young voice spoke in her defence, taking residence within his heart.

Yet, in his gut burned that bitter flame, the bailiff of the court that he could not fully reject. He felt a constant blade of unease in his skin and heard the whispers of the court in the shadows, their dark, formless faces casting their judgement upon him whenever he did glance at the corners, where silence slithered like a serpent.

VI

Despite what the court willed him to believe, the days appeared suspiciously animated after their first meeting. Though he was still bound strongly to his routines and daily rites, his heart and soul had been engulfed with a new-found fire, a curious matter that both pained and soothed his very core. Whenever they met, whether at the cafe or at the park, the court of his intellect remained unusually silent as if they had never held dominion over his mind and the young voice was the soul speaker in his mind. It was the sort of silence that, in the beginning, frightened him in a way he couldn't truly comprehend, but as time passed, so did his fears.

He was drawn to her eyes with a feeling one may call a passion, a thirst of curiosity, for her eyes indeed had a charming allure to them. Every day he found new details in them and learned new expressions of emotions from her. It was a rare moment when she was not blushing or smiling radiantly, yet when such a time came, it lasted only for a brief moment and seemed to him as if she was, for a second, stand-ing isolated in her own mind before returning to him as if it never happened. Perhaps one could consider this act strange, but he could do nothing but nod in understanding.

Even when he did not share his meal with her or hearken his ears to her words as they walked, he could still feel her warm spirit bringing light and warmth to his mundane existence, no matter if he sat writing in his usually gloomy office, or if he was attending his usual errand through the city. She was a new and constant force in his mind, a luminous moon, smiling upon him and slowly melting the ice around his heart, casting away the cloak of darkness he had heavily carried on his shoulders for as long as he could remember.

Yet with all the fresh passion and the new emotions, his intellect remained in part the same. The court may have remained silent for the majority of the time, but they still held firm to their judgement and whenever they gained a momentary dominance over the young voice, they burst into a venomous argument about her character. They first doubted her intent, her soul, her reasons for even looking upon a bitter old man like him. This initial doubt slowly grew into a full-on accusation, and whenever she was not present, the court wasted no time scrutinising her every gesture, her every formed word, her every glance.

In both her and his defence stood the young voice, coated in the passion of his heart, and though his voice remained strong and attuned with his growing affections for her, even the voice wavered, for the court had many voices, dark, treacherous, bitter. Thus, as the weeks turned into months and his life slowly took on a new form, he found himself slowly being torn between the two sides.

It was a cool autumn day when they had enjoyed an

evening in the park, adoring nature and the golden brown foliage all around them. The park was hushed with the soft rustling of the leaves and the sky was neither bright nor dark, simply serene in spirit and pleasant to the eye. They were sitting on the bench most familiar to him, for it was indeed his bench, his temporary throne, only now shared with her.

She shivered, for a sudden breath of the wind had whirled through them, hailing a scent of salt from the seas. Thus, he, contrary to the man he believed he was, had allowed her to press her head on his shoulder and enjoy the shelter of his coat.

Her smile was as pure as stars, her eyes sparkling with an innocence unknown in the fallen world of men. It cast a shiver through him as if a bolt of lightning had struck through his bones and brought down his spirit from whatever dark mountain he believed to live on. Emotions, burning and painful, bottled up in his throat and his chest thudded with the yawning of his heart. Her eyes seemed to see through him, through every dark crevice of his soul, and at that moment, he felt more bare than at the time of his birth. It was a moment that demanded a word, just a little word, perhaps a few words. They had to be whispered, spoken with a tongue only the heart could comprehend, cast into the wind who would then guide them to the other.

With the pressure mounting and his heart leaping like a strong deer, he narrowed his lips as to speak, yet all the sensations, the purity of her eyes, the burning flame in his skin, it all came to a halt as his intellect shouted and commanded him to freeze.

The court didn't give him a reason, but his words had

been snuffed out and for the rest of the day, the two of them merely sat together in silence. Yet there were words on his heart, inscribed with letters he did not know and the pain of not recognising them did not give him leisure.

She seemed to be her usual self, sighing longingly as she admired the trees and the birds above them, hopping on the canopies. Yet he remained shut, accustomed to the smile she had brought on his face. Yet his mind was steadily falling into turmoil and his spirit was restless, twitching and wavering like a flag on high. A blade had been thrust under his skin and he felt himself growing with an all-devouring dread, as if the world would come to a dark end at any given moment.

That day had come to an end with words of her hearty gratitude. They had come to her home once more, standing behind her door that suddenly hid her face from him, carefully calming her nervous breaths. It was then that she drew words from the secret chambers of her heart, presenting them to him with slightly teared-up eyes. He was very important to her. He had become a light in her life and she did not take his company for granted. Before he could conjure up a thought, before the court could mock her words and call her a liar, she leaned up and kissed his cheek, her lips soft as silk and sending a spreading fire all over his body.

The next thing he recalled was standing at the harbour, watching the uneasy movements of the sea. His cheek was still burning, his heart was tearing itself apart as it longed to rush back to her, and his soul was cascading into a vortex of despair, barred behind a calm, stoic face. He had glanced over his shoulder a few times after leaving her, as if to make sure she wasn't following him. Now that he was isolated, the court finally appeared up with their full might and removed the scales from his eyes.

Can you not see? She is making a mockery of you! You, sir Soren, you and a woman of that sort? Have you been wilfully blind or have you really turned mad?

The court was ruthless in their verdict and at that moment, as the sun was bowing its head behind the clouds, all the whispers of the court came to protest as one. He had not truly heeded their words since he had met her, but now, they revealed the obvious to him.

Is it a trick? A trick for your money? For your dignity? You know God delights in your torment, why should she be anything more than a hellish angel from His court? She has stolen your nature, your cadence, and look what she has done to you, tortured you by her smile. Woe is you, for you have indeed become a fool! This is not the first time we have told you this, yet it is obvious we must do so again, do not be fooled by the accursed wretch that beats in your chest.

Their judgement was harsher than any he had heard in his life. His face hardened, his figure hunched over, and what light had taken residence in his eyes was quickly evicted. Yet the young voice in his mind still spoke out in a vain hope to avoid the agony that was now becoming evident, but the court dismissed him all the same.

But, she seems so pure, innocent, dare I say beautiful, he thought.

Precisely. And you have let your guard down. You have become weak and allowed yourself to be defeated by Him. Open your eyes.

She is biding her time, like all of them do, waiting until you fully lower your guard before they smite you down and leave you for dead. Let it end, or this will surely annihilate you!

He clung his teeth together and held onto his heart, a pulsating pain radiating in his chest and turning numb his legs. His mind remembered her face, her eyes, that smile. That sweet, pure smile–that accursed smile! How could it be? Why would life torment him again? Why would God torture him again? As darkness clothed the world, his initial despair of the heart soon turned into wrath that boiled in every part of his being. It took all his might to keep him from roaring, from cursing the waters before him, but as the night went by, his heart eventually darkened. The court had issued their verdict and the trial was now over.

He limped home, his eyes hollow, his posture frail, his stride broken. His visage was akin to the shadows that lurked in the streets, his feet stirring the deadly silence of the city. Behind him was a trail of blood, of soul, of tears, and though his eyes were welling with unseen tears, his face did not even twitch. His true nature had finally defeated the stranger that had worn his skin for months and as stepped into his home, there came a moment of absolute silence, both in the realm of the physical, but also in the mind.

VII

Silence, a deceitful affliction of existence, a sting in the beating heart of man, crept around him. The morning was hesitant to arrive and the sun refused to grant its light, as if being an omen of dark tides.

Mr Soren stared blankly through the window and into the lifeless void, shadows nibbling on his vision. He had gotten no true rest in days, nor had he been spared from the constant barrage of empty thoughts and hollow emotions. He had been flogged, beaten, and tormented beyond measure by his own will, yet as the initial pain subsided, as the young voice in his mind died, he had come to accept the misery and to agree with it.

I was a fool. I shall not repeat my error, he thought.

With stiff movements, he prepared his pipe, cursing through his teeth as the tobacco fell from his grasp. The tobacco itself refused to be kindled and only after his rage had shown itself via the infernal hue on his face, did smoke arise from the pipe. Even when the preparations had been dealt with, the tobacco itself tasted sour, the unusual aroma he savoured being more akin to burned rubbish. Yet, he sat there as he always did, drew in the smoke as his face shuddered in disgust. His mind remained puzzled, but dead quiet, a sensation most strange and unnatural. His heart feared to beat and his body was a mere shell, without blood, without flesh, without a spirit; he felt weightless, yet bound to the earth as if by a curse.

The task of today was to end this foolish errand, this naive plot, this attempt of God to bring him to shame. His tongue had prepared the venom, and his eyes had sharpened the deadly gaze, yet when he carefully moved his lips as to speak, there still was something that kept him from even rehearsing the words he had chosen for her. His fingers tightened around his pipe. The chaos of his intellect turned maddening when suddenly her face revealed herself through the veil of his mind before quickly retreating into the depths. Then it came again with a flash and she sang to him with her damned sweet voice. He attempted to ignore her and keep her eyes from his own, yet she soon stared straight through him, her eyes sorrowful, welling, yet still shining with a sheen of warmth. His face lost its colour and his heart came to a halt, forcing him to gasp with a muffled voice. The apparition remained unchanging, leading him into a cycle of delusion until the court stood and demanded her to be exiled from his mind.

His pipe snapped into splinters. There came a sharp knock as it fell on the floor and with its terrible echo, he became still like a lake. Like a puppet, a cold wooden statue, he looked at his pipe and saw it lying there, full of sorrow and predestined death. The ashes had spread across the floor like seeds of wheat on a field and he could hear the quiet crackling of the flame, until it too faded into silence. It was time.

They had not met in a few days, but he had accepted her earlier proposal of meeting at the park once again. She had been ecstatic and deplorably more radiant than usual, revealing she had soon finished the piece she so wished to give to him. Her eyes had shimmered with a feigned innocence when she had spoken.

He could always merely send her a letter, but it would give another sign of his existence to her, a lasting sign. That wouldn't do. As he put on his cloak of darkness and hid his face under a hat, he froze to stare at himself in the mirror. Confusion took him and from the caverns of his soul shouted out a voice with a desperate and bloodied cry. Yet he could not make out the words and it faded under the weight of his mind. Nonetheless, he stood a while and studied the stranger he saw and nearly came to ponder if this was indeed him, yet he kept the thought from reaching its true form and left, in silence.

The world was breathless, grey, and tasteless. He felt himself being followed, as if someone was staring at him with blazing eyes, beckoning him to follow. As time passed, his features hardened and he was soon a sheer sculpture of his own figure, unanimated, harsh, and unreachable. It pleased his mind and as he gave himself to the thought, falling ever deeper into his darkened thoughts. His strange metamorphosis was finally at an end and he would soon rip off the root of his momentary agony.

He entered the park and heard the trees hushing one another in fear. Colour had faded from the park and the wind mounted the walls, bringing forth the cold news of approaching winter.

His eyes were sore to see her sitting where they–he had always sat. Her figure was still radiant, dressed in white with her hair gently wavering in the wind. She held her shivering hands and stared into a land unseen. It was only after he had nearly reached her that she flinched awake from thought and turned to greet him.

Immediately, confusion and a hint of fear rose on her face, threatening her usual smile while draining her of colour. She studied his eyes before observing him up and down before returning to his eyes.

She queried how he was, yet he would not even mutter out a response. She was embarrassed, yet her smile did not fade, only twitched. Her body trembled, as if she was anxious to reveal a word to him, yet now suddenly found herself unable to speak. Her eyes studied his own, seeking the man she had bid farewell to a few days ago, but it was then that her brows arched and her lips narrowed with a fright. The man she sought was not there.

Mr Soren?

Her voice made him flinch, for it still rang with a tune his ears could not but savour. Yet he hastily resumed his resolve and stared at her coldly. He was not to blame. It was she who attempted to fool him, a devil of God as she was. His tongue slithered, preparing to smite her, yet he hesitated, feeling a plug forming in his throat, suffocating him. Ye this momentary curse could not hold him for long and soon, he took action.

He turned deaf while his lips opened. Whatever he said

shot through her like a poisoned arrow, visibly shattering her and turning her figure feeble. She first rose to her feet, asking if he was alright. As she gained no reply, she began sobbing, her bright eyes fading into a dark and hopeless well. Her voice sank under her tears and she collapsed on the bench, hiding her face.

His tongue, his intellect, the remnants of his heart, none knew mercy. After he had spoken his will, the court relished in triumph, congratulating him with cold professionalism. He had spoken the last word, but as he was about to leave, there came in turn a whirling arrow at his back.

Through the tears, through the sobbing of a voice most pure, came the words, those accursed words crafted by God to act as a tormentor on his being.

I love you

He hesitated, his body afraid to take the next step. He wished to fall, for now in the crushing grip of the foulest agony. He stood still at the crossroads of time, between the roads of heaven and hell. His eyes were wide, seeing her in the dark that surrounded him and his heart let out a desperate cry. Her eyes were on him, calling out to him. Her sobs were a foul, excruciating torment in his ears, and the grip tightened around him, draining him of his breath. The remnants of the young voice rose up and spoke out to him, granting a vain plea to continue living in a lie, as the court noted. The world now turning hazy and his heart cold, he cut down the voice for the final time and sensed it fall to its final death.

He said a word. After came none. He heard her tears fading into the distance as his steps led him home. He faded into a timeless space where his memory had no power, where the world around him merely repeated itself in an endless contraption of meaningless architecture.

He then rid himself of all reminders of her existence. He burned her drawings, and her letters, and flogged his hands that had felt her warmth. After the purification of his life was complete, he returned to the truth of all existence; balance, control, and routine, the holy trinity resumed its dominance over all things and he followed this truth to the letter. For months he spoke not a word. For months he did not notice a true thought to appear in his mind. His intellect was silent, like a desolate land of ash and brimstone.

He wrote without recognising his writing. He ate without tasting the slightest aroma. He drew in the oppressed air and smelled no odours. He dreaded seeing a mirror, for there only a stranger greeted him.

Her smile faded from memory. Her words, her laughter, her warm hand on his own; it all joined the formless vapour that loomed over his very soul. There came a few nights when he dreamt of her, but immediately upon waking up, he convinced himself that indeed it was a mere nightmare and worked painfully to rid himself of the memory.

Hence, the life of Mr Soren descended to follow the worn tracks of rite and routine. There came no flashes of light, no sudden tears in the strict order that bound him, and no voices reached through the veil. Finally, his life had rid itself of falsehoods and returned to the truth. Yet there came a day when this long-retained stability was cast into doubt.

It was a grey day, just like the thousands that had come and gone, when Mr Soren sat in the grey corner of the grey restaurant he frequented for reasons even he did not know.

He opened the newspaper, thus breaking the holy sacrament of lunch for the first time in memory. It was then when a note, sorrowful in all sense, caught his eye. It was about the death of a local artist, a woman named Phoebe Ross.

It took some time and three readings for him to truly understand what the symbols on the paper meant, after which the gravity of the matter did not spare him. His heart leapt out of its prison and let out a cry of pain most sorrowful and his face stared blankly at the paper, his mind consumed by only a few words.

She is dead. She is dead? She is dead!

The court was nowhere to be seen, for they had no interest in following his destructive wave of regret. When he had fled home, he shouted, striking the walls while demanding the court to reveal themselves, to explain to him why he now felt as if a part of him had died with her. He brought his fist against the heavens and cursed God for his cruelty, for He had not only planted in him the seed of doubt, but also stolen her from him. He had once again succeeded in tearing down whatever life he had tried to conjure.

Yet after his rage faded, he heard the doorbell ringing. He did what he could to hide his madness and met a man who brought him a large frame, carefully wrapped in cloth.

He brought the frame inside, his heart in his throat and his tears burning his skin like molten steel. He drew aside the white cloth and gasped, falling on his back in horror, for it was the painting, the finalised painting of the drawing she had so earnestly, so lovingly, and so purely created.

In the frame was he, leaning on the railing and watching the sea, yet curiously clothed in light. His dark and callous face had been turned into a warm smile, emboldened by the moonlight, and on his face rested a peaceful, yet passionate smile. His eyes had been painted as if they too were a night sky, full of glimmering stars and a soul to bind them together. It was he, yet he could not believe it, for how could a living soul ever view him in such a manner? How could she have painted him so, when he was all but?

He cried a rebuke, a broken attempt of wrath, roared out in madness, yet his words were now truly in vain and the walls retreated from him. Not even his home stood by him and he slowly faded into an abyss he had believed to inhabit for so long.

The last light to fade from his home was the light in the painting, and with its death came, at last, silence.

The End